Published by Inhabit Media Inc.
www.inhabitmedia.com

Inhabit Media Inc. (Iqaluit) P.O. Box 11125, Iqaluit, Nunavut, X0A 1H0
(Toronto) 191 Eglinton Ave. East, Suite 301, Toronto, Ontario, M4P 1K1

Edited by Neil Christopher and Kelly Ward
Art direction by Danny Christopher
Design by Astrid Arijanto

We acknowledge the support of the Canada Council for the Arts for our publishing program.

This project was made possible in part by the Government of Canada.

ISBN: 978-1-77227-137-9

Printed in Canada.

Library and Archives Canada Cataloguing in Publication

Deal, Laura, author
     How Nivi got her names / by Laura Deal ; illustrated by
Charlene Chua.

ISBN 978-1-77227-137-9 (paperback)

     I. Chua, Charlene, 1980-, illustrator II. Title.

PS8607.E238H69 2016   jC813'.6   C2016-906706-8

How Nivi Got Her Names

By Laura Deal · Illustrated by Charlene Chua

Introduction

Many Inuit are born with a multitude of names, as opposed to the more common Western way of naming with a first name, middle name, and last name. I myself have five names, each of which is a name of a person who my parents cherished and respected. Through my names, I am the reincarnation of mothers, grandmothers, grandfathers, and beloved friends, most of whom have passed away. Through these names, I have a wide array of loved ones, connected not by blood, but by spirit.

For most, traditional naming is a way to keep a strong name from being lost, and to keep the spirit of our ancestors alive. Children named after important elders are spoken to with respect, and are treated the way that the elder once was. Sometimes, an elder will go to a pregnant woman and ask her to name her child after them. When a pregnant woman has a dream about an elder who has passed away, it is believed that the elder is asking for her child to be named after them.

There are many stories of children taking on the characteristics or qualities of those they are named after. At times, children grow up telling stories of their past lives, even though they were never told these stories by another person. There are other stories of children picking up objects that once belonged to their namesakes and saying, "This belongs to me." These could just be coincidences, but with Inuit mythology and the passing of knowledge through word of mouth over thousands of years, this seems unlikely.

An Inuit custom adoption is an adoption in which a pregnant woman provides her child to someone who needs a child. It could be a family member or another member of the community. In these adoptions, children grow up knowing who their biological family is and who their adoptive family is. Children can be adopted to their grandparents, and refer to their biological parent as a brother or sister, but they could also call each member of their family by their biological terms, as the child knows throughout their life how each person is connected. This has been practised for thousands of years. Traditionally, it ensured that when a couple could not have children, they would be provided one, and this would mean they could grow old and that the child would take care of them in their old age, in appreciation for being taken care of as a child.

Through a custom adoption, Niviaq became part of a large family that includes her two adoptive mothers—Jesse, her *anaana*, and Laura, her mom—her biological mother, me, and her biological father, David. Niviaq is part of the families of her two adoptive mothers, she is part of my family, and she is part of her biological father's family. Niviaq has four sets of grandparents who adore her and countless aunts, uncles, and cousins.

Through her names, Niviaq is a little girl, a grandfather, a grandmother, and a well-respected elder of all these families. And she's probably the cutest little girl in the whole universe.

—Aviaq Johnston

It was a beautiful but chilly spring morning, and instead of heading out into the cold, Nivi and her mom decided to play inside.

Nivi gave her mom her very best toy snowman and said, "You will be this one. What is its name, Mom?"

Nivi's mom looked at the toy and replied, "This one's name is Ikkii. You can be this one," she said as she handed Nivi a cute little stuffed pig. "She is named Kallak."

Nivi took Kallak from her mom's hand and made her hop around playfully, teasing Ikkii. "You'll never catch me! I'm cute and I'm Kallak!" Nivi called as she played. Then she stopped playing for a moment and thought to herself.

"My name is Niviaq," she said, pronouncing the *q* just as she had been taught to do. "But that's not my only name. My toys only have one name, but I have lots. I am Niviaq Kauki Baabi Irmela Jamesie. Those are my names!" Nivi stood up straight, proud to have recited all of her names perfectly.

"Why do I have so many names?" Nivi asked her mom.

Nivi's mom smiled. "When you were born, we knew we were going to name you Niviaq. We chose it as the special name we would call you because we knew we were adopting a little girl. Your name, Niviaq, means 'little girl.'

"There were lots of important people in our lives who meant a lot to our family," Mom added. "And you are named after some of those very special people."

Nivi sat next to her mother, very interested.

"In Inuit culture, people get their names from many different places, and some people, like you, have *many* names to be proud of. People are often named after family members and loved ones who are no longer with us. Babies, like you, are given the names of people who are no longer around so that their spirit and character can carry on in a new person. That is how traditional Inuit naming works," said Nivi's mom.

"But who am I named after?" Nivi asked.

"Let me try to explain. Because you were adopted from another family, you were given the name Kauki. Kauki was a special woman, the grandmother of your *puukuluk*, your birth mother. Kauki is no longer with us, but on the day you were born, when she first saw you, your birth mother was happily reminded of her dear grandmother. And so it made sense for us to call you Kauki, to honour her life and connect you in a special way to your biological family."

Nivi was very pleased to hear about Kauki, but she was excited to hear more. "What about Baabi?" Nivi asked.

"Baabi was an intelligent and kind soul," Nivi's mother said with a smile. "A man full of integrity and character and a special family friend. He appeared one night in a dream your *anaana* had. When she woke, she told Baabi's youngest daughter about her dream and asked if we could name our new baby after him once you arrived.

"Baabi's spirit and character live on through you, through your name. So his family—his wife and children—are connected to you because you are named after him. Baabi's sweet youngest daughter, whom you call Tissi, is your *panilaaq*. Tissi's mother, your *nuliarsuaq*, was Baabi's dear wife."

Nivi was really enjoying hearing about the special meaning of her names.

"Am I named after anyone else?" Nivi asked.

"Yes, *Panik*, you are named after my grandmother Irma, a resourceful and talented woman with great strength and creativity. She was a caretaker, my father's mother, and my loving gram." Nivi's mom paused and fixed Nivi's hair. "We named you Irmela after her so we can remember her, too."

All of the people sounded so wonderful. Nivi thought she would have liked them all very much. "And what about Jamesie?" asked Nivi.

"Jamesie was your anaana's grandpa," Nivi's mom replied. Nivi was listening very closely to her mother's words.

"Tell me more about him, Mom?" Nivi asked quietly. She looked at her mom with excitement and pride in her eyes.

"He was very special to your anaana—her favourite person." Nivi's mom paused and kissed Nivi on the head. "Until *you* were born," she told Nivi with a wink. "He was a generous man: traditional and very patient. Your anaana looked up to him very much and loved him very dearly," she said.

Nivi's mom paused. She then looked right at Nivi and said, "We all love you, dear Nivi, for all that you are. For the names that you have, for the character and traits we see in you, and the people we are reminded of when we are with you.

"Our hearts are filled with love, my panik! All of the people who love you and those who are connected to you through your names—me and your anaana, your puukuluk, your grandma, your panilaaq, your dear nuliarsuaq, your sons and daughters and grandchildren by your namesakes—we are all very proud of you and love you very, very much for many different reasons. Your names have brought us all together as a family . . . because of the love we share for you."

Nivi looked at her mom and gave her a big grin. "My names are very special, right, Mom?" Nivi asked.

"Your names are very special. And *you* are very special, my girl!" They shared a big, big hug and a *kunik*.

"You know what, Mom? I am proud of all of my names. Niviaq Kauki Baabi Irmela Jamesie!" Nivi said, very pleased.

Nivi and her mom played all morning until it was time for lunch. They sat together to eat *quaq* and macaroni and cheese in the warm afternoon sunshine.

It was a beautiful spring day.

About Inuit Kinship and Naming Customs

Traditionally, Inuit referred to one another using a system of kinship and family terms known as *tuqlurausiit*. Tuqlurausiit (Inuit kinship naming) fosters respect and closeness within families.

In Inuit culture, when a person dies, it is believed that their name, or name-soul, leaves the body and remains homeless until it is called back to take life again in the body of a newborn child. That child becomes known as an *atsiaq*, or "one who is called after." Traditionally, children were named after their elders or ancestors to ensure a long and healthy life.

A person's identity is closely associated with their name, and for this reason identities carry on when a new baby takes on a person's name. It is a common belief that a person's personality and character can be passed on from the dead to the living, and there is a sense that people are not naming a new person, but welcoming back a family member, a loved one, or a respected community member.

When names are shared and passed along in this way, personal relationships and social connections continue on, too. Traditional naming practices can connect many people and can strengthen community bonds.

In recent years, referring to one another by English names, as opposed to traditional kinship terms, has become more common, and the tradition of tuqlurausiit is slowly fading away.

It is important to keep this tradition alive for future generations. Sharing stories of kinship naming gives children the opportunity to understand important aspects of Inuit culture, to learn about the identities of those they are named after, and to discover the relationships that connect them to different generations.

Nivi's Namesakes

Kauki

Lizzie Kauki was the strength of her family and home. She did not know her own power. She enjoyed hunting, but relied on her guardian to hunt for her while she stayed behind and worked to clothe and feed the family. Kauki was an expert seamstress and always put her needs aside to help others and provide for her children. She did not want girls to be named after her for fear that they would go through the same hardships she did as a girl, because she was female. Out of respect for her wishes, Nivi was given Lizzie's last name, Kauki, instead of her female first name, because her family wanted to celebrate her strength and see that her name was passed on to other strong women.

(Written by Elisapee Johnston, Lizzie Kauki's daughter)

Baabi

Robert G. "Baabi" Williamson, who was born in England, was an anthropologist, Inuit advocate, and professor. He learned Inuktitut while living in Pangnirtung, Nunavut, in the 1950s and brought the first Inuktitut-language journal to the territory. He received numerous awards and honours throughout his career, including the Order of Canada in 1986. He was married to Greenlandic scholar Dr. Karla Jessen Williamson, with whom he had two children. Baabi also had four children from a previous marriage.

Jamesie

Jamesie Mike was born in Sarbarjua, near Pangnirtung, and he was eighty-four years old when he died. He had twelve children, over sixty grandchildren, and many great-grandchildren. He was a strong and resilient man, and a man of many talents; he was a hunter, a carver, and an engineer, and he kept a journal for decades recording and observing the weather. He was a sharer of knowledge and a loving and generous *ittuq* (grandfather). Because Nivi is named after him, she is an *ataata* (father), an ittuq, and an *amauq* (great-grandparent) to many people who love her because they are deeply connected to her through Jamesie's name.

(Written by Jesse Unaapik Mike, Jamesie's granddaughter)

Irma

Irma Fraser was born in a small farming community in rural Nova Scotia. She married and had four children. When her children were still young, she became a widow and opened up her home for boarders and transient workers passing through her community. As a single mom, she was a caregiver to many, a community volunteer, and a very hard worker. Irma used her talents in arts and crafts to help make ends meet and is remembered for her creativity and ingenuity.

Glossary

amauq	great-grandparent (a-mow-k)
anaana	mother (a-naa-na)
ataata	father (a-taa-ta)
atsiaq	one who is called after/named after (at-see-ak)
Ikkii	name, meaning "it's cold" (eek-key)
ittuq	grandfather (et-took)
Kallak	name, meaning "chubby" (cal-lack)
kunik	kiss (koo-nee-k)
Niviaq	name, meaning "little girl," Greenlandic origin, shortened from original (ne-vee-ak)
nuliarsuaq	big or great wife, Greenlandic origin (no-lee-ark-so-ak)
panik	daughter (pa-nick)
panilaaq	youngest daughter (pa-nee-lack)
puukuluk	biological mother (pooh-coo-look)
quaq	raw frozen meat or fish (co-walk)
tuqlurausiit	Inuit kinship naming (took-loo-ra-oo-seat)

About the Author and Illustrator

Laura Deal was born and raised in a small farming town in Nova Scotia. As a young adult, drawn to adventure, she climbed aboard an airplane for the first time ever and moved to Iqaluit, Nunavut. Laura immediately found appreciation for the culture, the beauty of the land, and the simplicity of Northern life. Since 2005, she has rooted herself in the Canadian Arctic and started a family. Niviaq is her three-year-old daughter who was adopted through Inuit custom adoption. A first-time author, Laura wrote this story for her daughter and dedicates it to her family and the extended family she has come to know through traditional custom adoption and kinship naming practices.

Charlene Chua worked as a web designer, senior graphic designer, web producer, and interactive project manager before she decided to pursue illustration as a career. Her work has appeared in *American Illustration*, *Spectrum*, and SILA's *Illustration West*, as well as several art books. She illustrated the children's picture books *Julie Black Belt: The Kung Fu Chronicles* and *Julie Black Belt: The Belt of Fire*, *Fishing with Grandma*, and *Leah's Mustache Party*. She lives in Toronto.

Acknowledgements

I wanted to write this book about kinship and extended families for many reasons. First, to show kids that families are defined by love and connection, each family being different in size and composition. Second, to help children learn about kinship connections and cultural naming practices so they are aware of this aspect of their culture and understand who they are and what makes them special.

Perhaps most importantly for me, I want my daughter and other children to have a strong sense of identity and to understand they are loved, respected, and supported by their families and communities. I hope that this story will help kids to understand their names and learn about identity, culture, and pride.

I would like to thank my Northern family members whom I have come to know through kinship naming and custom adoption—in particular, Aviaq Johnston and the Johnston family, Laakkaluk Williamson-Bathory and family, Karla Jessen Williamson, and Nivi's anaana, Jesse. Thank you all for showing me what it is like to be accepted into a new culture and how wonderful it is to be part of such a beautiful and unique extended family.

—Laura Deal